Little Devil Gets Sick

LITTLE DEVIL GETS SICK

By Marjorie Weinman Sharmat

PICTURES BY
Marylin Hafner

Doubleday & Company, Inc., Garden City, New York

For M.B.S.
My Favorite Devil
— M.W.S.

And Mine:
Abby, Jenny, Amanda
— M.H.

Library of Congress Catalog Card Number 79-7209

ISBN: 0-385-14209-9 Trade
ISBN: 0-385-14210-2 Prebound
Text copyright © 1980 by Marjorie Weinman Sharmat
Illustrations copyright © 1980 by Marylin Hafner

Library of Congress Cataloging in Publication Data

Sharmat, Marjorie Weinman.
  Little devil gets sick.

  (Reading-on-my-own book)
  SUMMARY: Little Devil unsuccessfully tries all sorts of nasty
things to help him get well. His cure eventually comes about, but
the reason for it is controversial.
  [1. Devil—Fiction] I. Hafner, Marylin.
II. Title.
PZ7.S5299Li   [E]

The sun set over Little Devil's house.
Little Devil was in bed.

"It is getting dark," he said.
"It is time to get up
and do a bad night's work.
I am going to make
a lot of trouble tonight!"

Little Devil yawned and stretched.
Then his nose started to run.
He sneezed and coughed.

"Drat! I don't feel well,"
he said. "I am sick.
Oh, am I sick!"

Little Devil lay under his quilts.

"I will get up
and cook some nice hot spider soup.
That always helps me
when I am sick."

Little Devil got out of bed.
He made some nice spider soup.

"This feels good
going down my throat," he said.

And he ate all the soup.
He turned on his television set.

"I will watch something
mean and nasty.
Then I will feel better,"
he said.

Little Devil watched
three programs in a row.
They were all
mean and nasty.

"I don't feel one bit better,"
Little Devil said.

He turned off the television set.

"Maybe I am not thinking
about this the right way,"
said Little Devil.
"Being sick can be cozy."

Little Devil lit
eight extra fires
in his fireplaces.

He took turns sitting
in front of each one.

"I feel cozy," he said.
"No, I feel awful.
I need help."

Little Devil heard
a knock at his door.

"Maybe someone has come
to help me," he said.

His friend Fritz
was at the door.

"Fritz, I am sick,"
said Little Devil.

"No wonder," said Fritz.
"It's those bad deeds you do.
They make you sick."

"Is that any way to talk
to a sick devil?"
asked Little Devil.

"I am sorry," said Fritz,
and he ran out.

Soon Fritz was back
with a bunch of roses.

"Sweet and pretty flowers
for a sick devil," said Fritz.

"Sweet and pretty flowers?"
said Little Devil.
"I hate sweet and pretty flowers!
They would make me sick
except I already am."

"No wonder," said Fritz.
"All those bad deeds."

He tossed the flowers
into the air
and left.

Little Devil called his mother.

"Mom, this is your son.
Your sick son," he said.

"You're sick?" said Mother Devil.
"Have you been doing good deeds?
That can make you very sick."

"Don't worry," said Little Devil.
"I have been very bad."

"Oh, good," said Mother Devil.

She rushed
to Little Devil's house.

"Now, did you try hot spider soup?"

"That is the first thing I tried,"
said Little Devil.
"It did not help.
I also tried blankets,
eight extra fires,
and mean and nasty television.
But I am still sick."

"Go back to bed,"
said Mother Devil.
"And wait for the darkest skies.
Wait for gloom, my son.
When that comes,
you will feel fine."

"That sounds like a good idea, Mom,"
said Little Devil.

Mother Devil tucked Little Devil
into bed and went home.
Little Devil waited for gloom.

But the night was bright
with a soft glow
from the moon.

"Turn off, moon!" cried Little Devil.

But the moon shone on.

"Please stop shining!"
shouted Little Devil.

Little Devil waited
and waited for gloom.
But it did not come.
At last he got out of bed.
He went to his desk.

"I must do something
to help myself," he said.
"I will make myself
a get-well card."

Little Devil painted a
dark and gloomy card.
GET WELL GLOOM, he wrote.
He put the card on his wall.

"And now for some get-well flowers,"
said Little Devil.

Little Devil went outside.

30

He shook his fist at the moon.
Then he pulled some weeds
from his weed garden.

He put them on his desk.
Then he looked at
his get-well card
and his get-well weeds.

"Now that I have all
these get-well things," he said,
"I should be getting well
right now."

Little Devil waited.

He sneezed.
He coughed.
His nose ran.

"I am still sick," said Little Devil.
"There is only one thing
left to do.
I will cast a spell on myself
and make myself well."

Little Devil flapped his cape.

He raised his arms.

"Oolie Oolie Zonka KOOOO!"
cried Little Devil.

Then he waited.

"Nothing is happening," he said.

"Maybe a plain spell
will work better."

Little Devil flapped his cape.
He raised his arms.

"Don't be sick.
Get well quick!" he cried.

Little Devil waited.
But nothing happened.

39

Little Devil sat
and thought.

"Maybe if I forget
I am sick,
I will remember
to be well," he said.
"I will go out
and be a well devil."

Little Devil sharpened his horns.
He oiled his pitchfork.

He ironed his devil suit.
He shined his cloven hoofs.

"Now I will go out
and make a lot of trouble."

Little Devil stepped out
into the moonlight.
He pretended it was not there.

Little Devil flapped his cape.
He raised his arms.

"Oolie Oolie Zonka KOOOO!"
he cried.

Little Devil turned
all the houses purple.

Then he wiped his runny nose.

"Drat! Purple houses make
my nose run faster," he said.

Little Devil flapped his cape.
He raised his arms.

"Oolie Oolie Zonka KOOOO!"

Little Devil turned all the trees
upside down.
Then he sneezed.

"Drat! Upside-down trees
make me sneeze harder."

Little Devil flapped his cape.
He raised his arms.

"Oolie Oolie Zonka KOOOO!"

Little Devil turned every rock
into a frog wearing glasses.

Then he coughed.

"Drat! Frogs with glasses
make me cough louder."

Little Devil was mad.

"It did not help to turn
houses purple
or trees upside down
or rocks into frogs."

Little Devil looked up at the moon.

"It is all your fault," he said.
"You with your cheery white light.
I will make you go away!"

Little Devil flapped his cape.
He raised his arms.

"Oolie Oolie Zonka KOOOO!" he cried.

But the moon kept shining.

Little Devil sneezed and coughed.
His nose ran.
He leaned against a tree.

"I must be the sickest devil
in the world," he said.

"No wonder!"
said a voice from the tree.
"All those bad deeds."

It was Fritz.

"You again?" said Little Devil.

"I know how you can
get well," said Fritz.

"How?" asked Little Devil.

"Do a good deed," said Fritz.

"A *what?*" cried Little Devil.

"A good deed," said Fritz.

"I never do good deeds!"
said Little Devil.

Little Devil sneezed and coughed.

"If I did a good deed,
what good deed would I do"
he asked.

"Put apples on all the trees
so people can make applesauce
whenever they want," said Fritz.

"That's dumb," said Little Devil.

But he stood up.

He flapped his cape.
He raised his arms.

"Oolie Oolie Zonka KOOOO!"

Little Devil turned all the trees
right side up
and they grew apples.

Then Little Devil waited for a sneeze.
He waited for a cough.
He waited for his nose to run.
Nothing happened.

"I am well!" cried Little Devil.
"Doing a good deed cured me!"

"I told you so," said Fritz.

They both ran to Little Devil's house.

Little Devil was so happy
he did not notice
that the moon had gone down.
The night was full of gloom.

Little Devil called his mother.

"Mom," said Little Devil.
"My nose does not run.
I don't sneeze or cough.
I am all better.
I did a good deed,
and it made me well."

"A *good deed?*" said Mother Devil.
"Why did you do
a terrible thing like that?
My son, you sound sicker than ever.
I am coming right over
with a month's worth
of hot spider soup."

"I don't need it,"
said Little Devil.

"You need it,"
said his mother.

Mother Devil left her house
with ten gallons
of hot spider soup.
Along the way,
she noticed that
the night was full of gloom.

"Aha!" she said.
"That is what cured my son.
A night of gloom
will cure anything."

When Mother Devil got to
Little Devil's house,
she pulled him to the window.

"See all that gloom," she said.

"I see it," said Little Devil.

"*That* is what cured you, my son,"
said Mother Devil.

"No!" said Fritz.
"The good deed did it."

"Gloom!!" said Mother Devil.

"Good deed!!" said Fritz.

Little Devil ran to a corner
and covered his ears.
He stayed there until
Mother Devil and Fritz went home.

Then he sat and thought.

"Drat! I don't know who
is right," said Little Devil.
"But just to be safe,
I will stay out of moonlight.
And I will do a very small good deed
now and then."

Little Devil went to bed.
Then he got up.

"There is one more thing
I will do," he said.

And Little Devil ate up
the whole month's worth
of hot spider soup.

THE
END